Here's what kids, parents, and teachers have to say to Ron Roy, author of the A to Z Mysteries series:

"Your books are my most prized possessions!"
—Sumedha R.

"Your books are great! I have just finished *The Orange Outlaw,* and you get two thumbs up!"—Patrick P.

"The A to Z Mystery books are filled with fun and excitement, and I can't seem to put them down."—Kelsey S.

"I will be so sad when I have read Z and there will be no more Dink, Josh, and Ruth Rose."—Jack P.

"As a parent, I like your books because they show kids using their brains and doing the right thing."—Carla C.

"The excitement for reading that you have helped create is a blessing! One boy said his mother doesn't know what has gotten into him because he constantly has a book in his hands. Now, if that isn't a teacher's dream!"—Tamela K.

The R book is dedicated to readers.
—R.R.

To author and horse lover Jessie Haas.
—J.S.G.

Text copyright © 2002 by Ron Roy
Illustrations copyright © 2002 by John Steven Gurney
All rights reserved under International and Pan-American Copyright
Conventions. Published in the United States by Random House
Children's Books, a division of Random House, Inc., New York,
and simultaneously in Canada by Random House of Canada Limited, Toronto.

www.randomhouse.com/kids
www.ronroy.com

Library of Congress Cataloging-in-Publication Data
Roy, Ron.
The runaway racehorse / by Ron Roy ; illustrated by John Steven Gurney.
p.   cm. — (A to Z mysteries)
SUMMARY: Dink, Josh, and Ruth Rose investigate the disappearance of a
valuable racehorse that Dink's uncle and his friend, Forest Evans, have just
bought and entered in a race at Saratoga.
ISBN 0-375-81367-5 (trade) — ISBN 0-375-91367-X (lib. bdg.)
[1. Race horses—Fiction. 2. Horses—Fiction. 3. Larchmont (N.Y.)—Fiction.
4. Mystery and detective stories.]   I. Gurney, John, ill. II. Title.
PZ7.R8139 Ru 2002   [Fic]—dc21   2002002726

Printed in the United States of America   First Edition
20 19 18

RANDOM HOUSE and colophon and A TO Z MYSTERIES are registered
trademarks and A STEPPING STONE BOOK and colophon and the
A to Z Mysteries colophon are trademarks of Random House, Inc.

A to Z Mysteries®

The Runaway Racehorse

by Ron Roy

illustrated by
John Steven Gurney

A STEPPING STONE BOOK™

Random House 🏠 New York

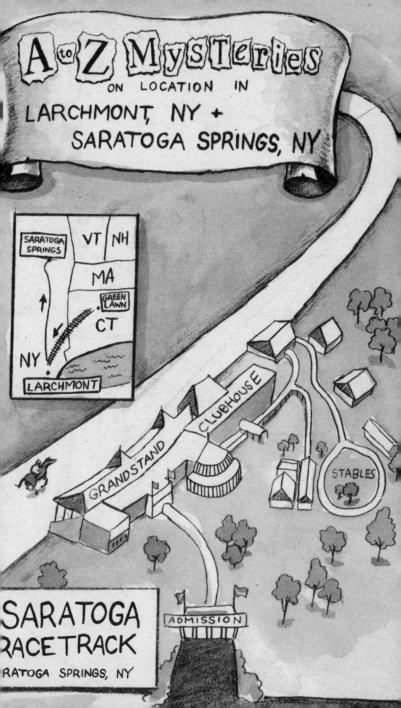

CHAPTER 1

Josh picked up a French fry, dipped it in ketchup, and drew his initials on his plate. When he ate the French fry, a glob of ketchup plopped onto his shirt.

"Rats, this is my favorite T-shirt!" Josh said.

Dink put down his book and grinned at his freckle-faced, redheaded friend. "*Was* your favorite shirt," he said.

Josh, Dink, and Ruth Rose were taking a train to Larchmont, New York, to visit their friend Forest Evans. Forest and Dink's uncle Warren had bought a

1

racehorse together. The kids were invited to watch the horse, Whirlaway, run in a race in Saratoga Springs.

Josh picked up a napkin and wiped at the red stain. He only made it worse.

"Josh is finger-painting," Ruth Rose said to Dink.

"Someday I'll be a famous ketchup artist," Josh said. He gazed out the window. "When do we get there?"

"In a few minutes," Ruth Rose said, checking her train schedule.

"I can't wait to see Whirlaway," Dink said. "I've never met a real racehorse before. All I can think about is horses! That's why I'm reading this."

He held up his book. It was *The Black Stallion* by Walter Farley. The cover showed a beautiful black horse with wild eyes and a flowing mane.

Dink Duncan's real first name was Donald, and his middle name was David. But when he first started to talk and tried to say "Donald David Duncan," it came out as "Dink." Dink had been his nickname ever since.

"Look what I brought," Ruth Rose said, pulling a book from her backpack. The cover showed a girl on a horse. The book's title was *Learning to Ride*.

"Josh, did you bring a horse book?" Dink asked.

Josh grinned. "Nope. I figured you guys will tell me anything I need to know." He dropped a few sugar cubes into his backpack.

"Still hungry?" Dink teased.

"They're for Whirlaway," Josh said.

Just then the conductor walked through the dining car. "Larchmont is next," he told the kids.

"Oh, wait!" Ruth Rose said, digging in her backpack. She brought out her new camera.

Ruth Rose liked to dress all in one color. Today everything was white, from her headband down to her sneakers. Even her camera was white!

"Would you please take our picture?" she asked the conductor.

"My pleasure," said the man. He took the camera and focused it on the kids. "Say 'cheese'!"

"Cheese!" they all said.

The conductor handed Ruth Rose her camera. "Have a great day," he said.

The train slowed, then stopped. Dink, Josh, and Ruth Rose grabbed their backpacks and walked to the end of the car. The conductor lowered a set of stairs, and the kids climbed down to the platform.

Dink heard someone call his name. He saw his uncle Warren and Forest Evans walking toward them. Dink's uncle was short and round and wore glasses. Forest Evans had a trimmed brown beard and wore jeans and a T-shirt.

"Why, it's Wink, Gosh, and Tooth Toes!" Forest said.

The kids had met Forest when his painting had gotten stolen from Uncle Warren's apartment.

"Hi, Mr. Evans!" they all said.

"Please call me Forest, okay?" he asked.

TRACK 5

Dink hugged his uncle.

"How was the train ride?" Uncle Warren asked.

"Great!" Josh said. "The hamburgers were awesome!"

Forest led them to a black car and opened a rear door. The kids piled in with their backpacks. Uncle Warren sat next to Forest up front. Forest started the car and pulled out of the parking lot.

"How many horses do you have?" Josh asked.

"Just Whirlaway," Forest said.

"Do you ride him in races?" Ruth Rose asked.

Forest laughed. "No, I'm too heavy. Professional jockeys are small and light. I hired a woman named Sunny to be Whirlaway's jockey."

"Awesome!" Josh said. "I've never met a girl jockey before." Then he added, "I've never met a boy jockey, either."

Forest slowed down near a group of small shops and flipped on his turn signal. Dink, Josh, and Ruth Rose recognized the long, tree-lined driveway. They had been here once before with Dink's uncle.

A minute later, Forest stopped at his garage. At the end of a stone path stood a large brick house. Out back a stone barn nestled between a tennis court and a swimming pool.

"Here we are," Forest said.

The kids climbed out of the back-seat with their backpacks.

"When can we meet Whirlaway?" Josh asked, looking toward the barn.

"Right now!" Forest said.

Uncle Warren headed to the house while the kids followed Forest toward the barn.

Josh dug in his pocket and pulled out a sugar cube. "I brought this for Whirlaway," he said.

"That was a nice idea, Josh," Forest said. "But Whirlaway doesn't like sugar. He's the only horse I've seen who doesn't!"

Josh stuck the cube back in his pocket as the kids entered the cool, dim barn. Dink took a deep breath. "It smells nice in here," he said.

"I agree," Forest said. He also took a deep breath. "There's nothing like the sweet smell of hay and horse."

"Don't forget chocolate," Josh added.

They all laughed as Forest led the way to a stall near the barn's rear doors. The doors were open and sunlight poured in. Out back was a truck parked on a wide area of gravel.

The stall door was also open, but there was no horse inside.

"That's funny," Forest said, closing the stall door. He thought for a moment, then smiled.

"I'll bet Sunny took Whirlaway out for exercise," he said. "They should be back soon. Let's go get you guys settled in the house."

He led Dink, Josh, and Ruth Rose back outside and into the house. They passed through a small room with boots on the floor and jackets hanging on pegs.

"This is the mudroom," Forest said,

untying and kicking off his boots.

He took the kids through another door into the kitchen. The room was yellow with blue tiles on the counter and floor.

Forest pointed to a low bench. "You can leave your backpacks there for now," he said.

The kids stood their packs on the bench. Dink glanced at a newspaper clipping stuck to the refrigerator door with a magnet. There was a picture of a dark horse with a diamond-shaped blaze on his forehead. The headline read LOCAL HORSE BEATS ALL.

"Is that Whirlaway?" Dink asked.

"That's him," Forest said.

"He's real pretty," Ruth Rose said.

"He's even prettier in person," Forest said, opening the fridge. "You kids like fruit?"

"We like *everything*!" Josh said.

Forest set grapes and strawberries

on the table. The kids sat down and began to snack.

Suddenly the door burst open. A small woman in jeans, riding boots, and a flannel shirt rushed into the kitchen.

"Hi, Sunny," Forest said. "Say hello to Dink, Josh, and Ruth Rose. They're here to watch you and Whirlaway race tomorrow."

"He's gone!" Sunny said, trying to catch her breath.

"Who's gone?"

"Whirlaway!" she said. "I just got here to take him out. When I looked in his stall, it was empty!"

CHAPTER 2

Forest looked up in surprise. Then suddenly, his face relaxed.

"Don't worry, I'll bet Whirlaway went to visit his mother again," Forest said. "I'll call Mr. Bunks."

"Who's Mr. Bunks?" Ruth Rose asked.

"Tinker Bunks owns the ranch next to my property," Forest said. "He tried to raise horses for racing. He never had much luck, so he sold off his stock. That's how Warren and I got Whirlaway. Mr. Bunks kept Whirlaway's mother, a nice old mare named Biscuit."

"How does Whirlaway visit his mother?" Dink asked.

Sunny frowned. "The rascal gets out of his stall and cuts through the woods," she said.

"I wonder when he got out this time," Forest said. "He was here this morning when Warren got here. We went in and visited him."

"So he could have been gone all day!" Sunny said.

Forest nodded slowly. "Yes, it's possible, Sunny. But let's not worry. Last time he ran away, I found him safe and sound, munching hay with his mother."

Forest reached for the phone and dialed. He listened, then hung up.

"Mr. Bunks's line is busy," he said. He looked at the kids. "If you're finished, why don't we jump in my truck and take a ride over there?"

"I'll throw down some fresh straw in Whirlaway's stall," Sunny said. She headed out the door toward the barn.

Forest put the fruit back in the fridge and the kids followed him out the kitchen door.

He led them to the gravel parking area behind the barn. Forest's pickup truck was filled with bales of hay.

"Who wants to ride in the back with the hay?" Forest asked.

"I do!" Josh said.

"I will, too," Ruth Rose said. "Otherwise, Josh will be scared."

"Just make sure you hang on," Forest said. "We're taking the old logging road through the woods and it's pretty bumpy."

Ruth Rose and Josh scrambled into the truck's bed and sat on hay bales. Dink climbed into the cab next to Forest.

Forest started the truck and drove into the trees. Dink bounced in his seat as the tires rolled over bumps in the road. Low branches brushed the top of the cab.

Dink turned around to look through the rear window. Josh and Ruth Rose were laughing and holding on to the sides of the truck.

A few minutes later, they came out of the woods. Up ahead Dink saw a barn and a house. Forest pulled into the driveway and stopped behind another truck.

A dog was tied to a nearby tree. He leaped up and started barking.

"Calm down, Buster," Forest said out his window. "Be a good dog."

A man came from behind the barn. He was wearing a work shirt, jeans, and a leather belt with a big silver buckle. Muddy rubber boots came up nearly to his knees.

"Lie down, Buster," the man said. Buster stopped barking and flopped down on the ground.

"Afternoon, Tinker," Forest said.

Tinker Bunks walked over and leaned on the door. He had a thin face, sharp blue eyes, and thick brows.

"Good day to you, Forest," he said. "That horse I sold you still running like the wind?"

Forest nodded and smiled. "He's won every race so far," he said.

"Winnin' is good," Mr. Bunks said. He looked off into the distance for a few seconds. "But I'm glad the racing business is behind me now. A lot of work, horses."

He peered into the cab. "So what brings you here today?"

"I'm afraid Whirlaway has disappeared again," Forest told Mr. Bunks. "Any chance he's come to visit his mother?"

Mr. Bunks arched his eyebrows. "Not so far as I know," he said, glancing toward the barn. "Let's go have a look."

The kids followed Mr. Bunks and Forest into a large barn. As they entered, Dink heard a horse whinny. "We hear you, Biscuit," Mr. Bunks said.

The barn was cool and dim. Dust hung in the air where sunlight came through high windows. A loft held rows of hay bales. The floor was swept clean.

Dink peeked into several stalls. Each was clean and empty.

Mr. Bunks stopped at a stall with its

top door open. A pale brown horse with dark eyes stood there waiting. She had a small white mark on her forehead.

"This is Whirlaway's mom," Forest told the kids. He patted Biscuit on her nose.

"Have you seen your son today, old girl?" Mr. Bunks asked his horse.

As if she understood, Biscuit shook her large head from side to side.

"I thought for sure he'd be here," Forest said. He peered into a few of the empty stalls.

"I'm afraid I've wasted your time," Forest told Mr. Bunks. "Come on, kids. It's time to call the police."

CHAPTER 3

Tinker Bunks looked serious. "If he shows up, I'll give you a shout."

"I'd appreciate that," Forest said. "He's running at Saratoga tomorrow."

"Is he now!" Mr. Bunks said. "I wish you luck."

They all left the barn. The sky had grown darker. As Forest drove through the woods, Dink heard thunder. Wind began to whip tree branches back and forth.

Forest drove faster. "I'd better get us home before Josh and Ruth Rose have a shower!" he said.

Forest parked behind his barn just as raindrops began to splatter the windshield. "Let's run for it!" he said, leaping from the cab.

Dink, Josh, and Ruth Rose ran, squealing, as the clouds opened up. In seconds they were soaking wet.

Inside the house, Forest handed them towels. They dried their hair and faces.

"Why don't you settle in while I call the police," he said. "Ruth Rose, you're in the blue bedroom. Guys, you're bunking right across the hall."

The kids grabbed their backpacks and headed toward the back of Forest's house. Ruth Rose stopped outside a bedroom with blue wallpaper.

"See you guys in a minute," she said, and disappeared inside.

Dink and Josh walked into their room and changed into dry shirts.

A minute later, Ruth Rose knocked

and came in. Her wet hair was even curlier than usual.

"What could have happened to Whirlaway?" she asked Dink and Josh.

Dink looked out the bedroom window. Through the rain, he could see the barn. But he couldn't see the barn's rear doors.

"You know, someone could have stolen him," Dink said.

"Stolen him!" Josh said. "In broad daylight?"

Dink pointed. "You can't see the back doors of the barn from the house," he said. "Anyone could go in and out that way."

Ruth Rose peered through the streaming window. "How would you steal a horse?" she asked. "Would you need a trailer?"

"Or the thief could just ride him away," Josh said.

"Let's go look behind the barn for

clues when the rain stops," Ruth Rose said.

"Maybe the police had some good news for Forest," Dink said.

They headed for the kitchen.

Forest was also staring out the window into the rain. His shoulders were hunched, and he was nervously tapping his fingers on the counter.

Uncle Warren was sitting at the table, drinking a mug of tea.

"Did you call the police?" Dink asked.

Forest turned away from the window and nodded. "Yes. They told me no one's called in about a stray horse," he said. "I'm getting worried."

"Do you think someone might have stolen him?" Dink asked.

Forest looked at him and blinked a few times. "Stolen Whirlaway? I suppose it's possible."

"Forest, have you any neighbors

who own horses?" Uncle Warren asked.

"A few, why?"

"Because Whirlaway may not be the only missing horse," Uncle Warren said. "Perhaps you should call around."

"Good idea. I will," Forest said.

"We'll help you look for him when the rain stops," Ruth Rose said.

Forest nodded. "That'll be great. Now I'd better get on the phone," he said as he left the kitchen.

The kids drank milk and ate cookies with Uncle Warren. They watched the rain streak down the windows.

Forest came back a few minutes later. "I called two friends who own horses," he said. "None are missing, but my friends said they'd keep an eye out for Whirlaway."

The rain continued. They played Scrabble. When it wasn't his turn, Forest kept jumping up to call more neighbors.

Finally the rain stopped and the clouds cleared. When Dink looked out the window, sunlight sparkled off trees and bushes.

"I'll go pick up some food for dinner," Uncle Warren said. He took a set of car keys from a hook and left the house.

"Okay, kids, let's go look for my horse," Forest said.

He and the kids put on sneakers and headed through the kitchen door to the yard. The wet grass squished under their feet.

They walked behind the barn. Forest headed toward the woods, whistling and yelling, "Whirlaway!"

Dink, Josh, and Ruth Rose checked the wet ground for tire tracks or footprints.

"Nothing," Josh muttered. "Even if there *were* clues, the rain washed them away."

Suddenly the kids heard a soft whinny from inside the barn.

Dink yelled for Forest, who came running.

"Whirlaway?" Forest said. They all ran into the barn.

Standing outside Whirlaway's stall was a wet, muddy horse.

"Where have you been, boy?" Forest asked his horse.

Whirlaway shook his head. Water and mud flew off his mane. He stomped his front foot and gazed at the humans.

Forest walked over and grasped Whirlaway's halter. It, too, was muddy.

Forest laughed and shook his head. "Looks like you've been rolling in a big mud puddle," he said. "Kids, do you know how to wash a horse?"

"Yes," Josh said. "We wash my pony all the time."

Forest pointed to a hose and some buckets and sponges. He handed Ruth Rose a container of green soap. "Just be careful of his feet," he said.

Forest snapped a leather lead onto Whirlaway's halter, then hooked the other end to a post. "Rinse the mud off first, then soap him down good."

Just then they heard a phone ringing from the house. "I'd better get that," Forest said. "When Whirlaway is dry, just put him back in his stall." He hurried back to the house.

Dink filled a bucket with water, then turned the hose on Whirlaway. The horse stood still as muddy water cascaded off his sides.

Ruth Rose poured some soap into the bucket, making the water turn green. The suds smelled like freshly cut grass.

The kids soaked three big sponges in the soapy water. They each began washing a different part of the horse. Whirlaway rolled his eyes and tried to watch all three kids.

"Hey, look at this," Josh said. He pointed to the horse's side. There was a mark in the mud. It was egg-shaped, about as big as his hand. Inside the oval was some kind of wiggly shape.

"Josh, have you been finger-painting again?" Ruth Rose teased.

"I didn't do that!" Josh said. "It was already there."

The three kids looked closely at the imprint.

"It almost looks like someone stamped him with something!" Josh said.

CHAPTER 4

"Whirlaway could have gotten that when he was rolling in the mud," Dink said. "He probably rolled over a rock or piece of wood."

"Yeah, probably," Josh said. He wiped his soapy sponge over the strange sign and it disappeared.

Dink trained the hose on Whirlaway again to rinse off the soap.

Ruth Rose found some towels hanging on the wall, and they rubbed Whirlaway's coat.

When he was dry and shining, Ruth Rose unhooked Whirlaway's lead from the post to put him in his stall. "Come on, boy," she said.

Whirlaway rolled his eyes at Ruth Rose. He stiffened his legs and refused to walk.

"Good job, kids!" Forest said as he walked into the barn. "He looks like a new horse!"

"He won't go in his stall," Ruth Rose said.

"Let me try," Forest said. He took the lead from Ruth Rose and began stroking Whirlaway's neck. He spoke softly in the horse's ear. After a minute, Whirlaway walked into his stall. He stuck his nose into the oats bucket and began eating.

Forest closed the stall door behind Whirlaway. "He was probably a little spooked from being out during the storm and coming home to all these strangers," he said.

Just then Sunny rode through the

barn's rear doors on a mountain bike. She hopped off, leaned the bike against a wall, and strode over in tall, muddy boots. "There's the bad boy," she said, reaching over the stall door to pet his nose.

Whirlaway rolled his eyes, threw his head up, and backed into a corner.

"Easy, boy," Sunny murmured. She looked at Forest. "He seems scared of me."

"He did the same thing with me," Ruth Rose said.

The five humans watched the horse, who was also watching them.

"Maybe he doesn't feel good," Dink suggested.

"Could he have eaten something bad while he was gone?" Josh asked.

"It's possible," Forest said. "But he looks fine. And he just ate some oats."

Sunny studied the horse. "I hope he runs okay tomorrow."

"How far away is Saratoga?" Dink asked.

"A few hours. It's near Albany," Sunny told him. She looked at Forest. "I'll come over at six and load Whirlaway into the trailer. I'll be there in plenty of time for him to relax before his race."

"Good," Forest said. "Now let's go see what Warren bought for our supper."

Forest looked at his horse. "No more disappearing tricks, fella," he said.

Sunny pulled the stall's top door shut and checked that the latch was in place.

"See you tomorrow in Saratoga," she said. The kids watched her straddle her mountain bike and ride out the door. She looked funny pedaling a bike in muddy rubber boots.

Uncle Warren was back with groceries. Soon they were all eating a hearty meal. After supper, they finished the Scrabble game.

At nine o'clock Forest stood up and yawned. "Long day tomorrow," he said. "I'm ready to turn in."

"Sounds good to me, too," said Uncle Warren. "See you all in the morning." He patted Dink on the head and left the room.

The kids padded down the hall to

their rooms. As Dink and Josh were crawling into their beds, they heard a knock.

Ruth Rose opened the door. "Nice Daffy Duck jammies, Josh," she said, marching into the room with her book.

"Quack-quack," Josh said.

Ruth Rose sat on the end of Dink's bed with the book on her lap. "I want to read you guys something," she said.

"Oh, goody," Josh said. "Can we have milk and cookies, too?"

Ruth Rose held up her book. "This is really about learning to ride your own horse," she said. "But there's a chapter about jockeys."

She opened the book and began reading: *"Jockeys must earn the horse's trust. A good jockey does this by feeding and grooming the horse regularly. Most horses learn to like their jockeys and become friends."*

Ruth Rose looked up from the page. "Does anything strike you about that?" she asked.

"Like what?" said Josh.

"Well, did you notice how Whirl-away acted around Sunny?" Ruth Rose said.

"He sure didn't seem very friendly to her," said Dink.

"Yeah, he backed away as soon as she came in," said Josh.

"Exactly," Ruth Rose said. "I think Whirlaway's *afraid* of Sunny!"

CHAPTER 5

A hand on his shoulder woke Dink from a sound sleep. The light next to his bed was on. *The Black Stallion* lay on the bedcovers, still opened.

Through sleepy eyes, he looked into his uncle's face.

"Morning, Donny," Uncle Warren said quietly. "Time to get up."

"Hi, Uncle Warren," Dink said.

"You boys have to hop to it," Uncle Warren said. "Forest wants to get on the road right after breakfast." He smiled at Dink and left the room.

Dink tossed his pillow over at Josh's

bed, then walked into the bathroom. Josh grumbled, but soon they were both dressed and headed for the kitchen.

Forest and Ruth Rose were sitting at the table eating oatmeal. Uncle Warren took a pot off the stove and filled bowls for Dink and Josh.

"Everyone sleep all right?" Forest asked.

"I did," Ruth Rose said. She spooned some brown sugar over her cereal. Today her color was purple: purple leggings, purple blouse, purple headband, purple sneakers.

"Me too," Dink said. "Except for Josh's snoring all night."

They ate quickly, then left the house and piled into Forest's car. Dink, Josh, and Ruth Rose sat in the backseat. They each had their books, and Josh had brought his pillow.

Forest turned out of his driveway and drove through Larchmont. After making a few turns, he was on a wide highway. Dink saw a sign that said ALBANY, 120 MILES.

A few hours later, they arrived in Saratoga Springs. Forest pulled his car into a parking lot.

They all climbed out of the car and stretched their legs. Under tall trees, Dink saw long green barns. Near the barns, men and women were grooming horses, feeding horses, exercising horses. There were horses everywhere!

Ruth Rose took pictures of horses and one of a barn with the sun shining on the green wood.

"Let's go find Sunny," Forest suggested. "She'll be in barn E. Stall number twenty-one."

They cut through some trees, following a wide path. Barns stood on both sides of the path. Each barn had a large letter painted on one side.

The gravel walkway was crowded
with people. Some were walking horses;
others were just looking.

"There's barn E," Josh said, sprinting
ahead.

Forest, Uncle Warren, and the kids
found Sunny outside stall 21. She had
one foot on a bale of hay and was

buffing her riding boot with a cloth. A
can of black boot polish sat on the floor.

"Hi, Sunny," Forest said.

Sunny wore white riding pants. Her
silk racing shirt was green with yellow
stripes on the arms. Circling her left
arm was a cloth band with the number
21 stitched on. Her hair was tucked up

under a hard hat covered in yellow silk. Oval-shaped goggles rested on the hat's visor.

Sunny dropped the cloth and smiled. "Hi, everyone," she said.

"Any problems?" Forest asked.

"He didn't want to walk into the trailer this morning," Sunny said. "And he *definitely* didn't like me getting him ready once we got here."

"Good morning, Whirlaway," Forest said to his horse. "Why are you giving Sunny a hard time, eh, boy?"

Everyone peered into the stall. Whirlaway was standing in a corner with his eyes on the newcomers.

"He looks terrific, Sunny," Forest said. "Nice job."

Sunny had brushed Whirlaway's coat till it gleamed. The white tape she'd wrapped around his ankles looked snowy against his nearly black coat.

"Why do you wear goggles?" Ruth Rose asked Sunny.

"To protect my eyes," Sunny said. "During races, the horses in front of me kick up dirt. You should see me when I race in the rain. Totally covered in mud!"

"What time is the race?" Dink asked.

"We're in the second one," Sunny said. "Two o'clock."

"We'll be cheering you on," Uncle Warren said.

"Can I take a picture of you and Whirlaway?" Ruth Rose asked.

"Sure," Sunny said. She walked into the stall and put her hand on Whirlaway's halter. Whirlaway rolled his eyes at her and threw his head back.

Ruth Rose is right, thought Dink. *Whirlaway doesn't like Sunny at all.*

Ruth Rose snapped a picture.

CHAPTER 6

"Okay, gang, let's go grab our seats," Forest said.

To get to Forest's private box, they had to climb up three flights of stairs. Throngs of people filled the grandstand. Music was playing, and everyone seemed to be having a good time.

The viewing box had a row of seats under a little roof. On both sides were other private boxes. Straight ahead was a perfect view of the starting gate and oval racetrack.

"How long is the race?" Josh asked.

"Twice around the track," Forest said.

A stack of race programs was on one seat. Forest handed them out. "Whirlaway's on page two," he said.

The kids quickly checked and found Whirlaway's name. Sunny was listed as Whirlaway's jockey.

"This is so exciting!" Ruth Rose said. She set her camera on the floor under her chair.

A waiter wearing a white jacket came and took their lunch order. They made it simple for him: five cheeseburgers, five lemonades.

"Where do the horses end up?" Josh asked.

"At the finish line," Uncle Warren said, "down there behind the starting gate."

The waiter brought their food. As they ate, they watched a group of horses and their riders come out onto the track. Some of the horses were bucking and prancing. The jockeys were outfitted in bright colors. Each rider wore goggles like Sunny's.

The horses were white, gray, black, and several shades of brown. One was a golden palomino.

Down below the owners' boxes, people were lined up along the track fence. They began cheering when they saw the horses at the starting gate.

Suddenly a man's voice came over the speakers. "GOOD AFTERNOON, LADIES AND GENTLEMEN!" he cried. "THE FIRST RACE IS ABOUT TO BEGIN!" While he called out the names of the horses and jockeys, the riders moved their horses up to the starting gate.

Then a loud bell sounded, and the horses burst onto the track. The jockeys stood in the stirrups, their heads bent low over the horses' necks.

The crowd shouted and cheered. Even above the noise, the kids could hear the thunder of the horses' hooves on the track. Clumps of dirt flew into the air behind each horse.

"AND IT'S MERRY MARY IN THE LEAD!" the announcer exclaimed. "STARBURST IS A LENGTH BEHIND! CRANBERRY SAUCE IS THIRD!"

Then it was over. A white horse had rocketed across the finish line first.

"AND IT'S MERRY MARY BY HALF A LENGTH!" yelled the announcer.

As the kids watched, the jockey pranced Merry Mary to the winner's circle. A woman wearing a dress and a wide hat presented the jockey with a trophy. A man in a suit beamed and posed for a picture. "That's the horse's owner," Forest informed the kids.

"Is our race next?" Dink asked, checking his program.

"Yes, in just a few minutes," Forest said. He pointed to the track. "The horses are coming out already."

The three kids stood up.

"Which one is Whirlaway?" Ruth Rose said, getting her camera ready. "There are a lot of dark horses with white marks on their foreheads."

Forest pointed over her shoulder. "In front of the white horse," he said. "See Sunny's yellow hat? And you can see the big twenty-one on Whirlaway's saddle blanket."

The horses and riders approached the starting gate. When the announcer shouted, "NUMBER TWENTY-ONE IS WHIRLAWAY, RIDDEN BY SUNNY FIELDS!" Dink, Josh, and Ruth Rose cheered. Ruth Rose snapped a picture. Forest put two fingers in his mouth and whistled.

Then the announcer's voice boomed over the loudspeakers. "NOW THE SECOND RACE! AN EVEN DOZEN BEAUTIES OUT THERE!"

And then the starting bell sounded, and the race was on. The crowd began yelling, but didn't drown out the announcer's voice.

"WHAT A SIGHT, FOLKS! FANCY PANTS IS OUT FRONT. HIGH FIVE IS NEXT! HERE COMES PRETTY BALLOON ON THE OUTSIDE! AND LOOK AT THIS. DANCER IS SNEAK-ING UP ON PRETTY BALLOON. HE'S PASSING HIGH FIVE. DANCER IS IN THE LEAD!"

Dink, Josh, and Ruth Rose were on their feet. They jumped and yelled, "Come on, Whirlaway!"

But Whirlaway was nowhere near the front. Number 21 was second to last as the horses barreled toward the finish line.

By the time the race was over, Whirlaway had fallen back even more. He came in dead last.

The kids sat down, disappointed. Forest stared at the racetrack.

"What happened?" Uncle Warren said.

Forest shook his head. "Whirlaway has never run so badly," he said. "There's something wrong!"

CHAPTER 7

"Well, he tried," Uncle Warren said, laying his hand on Forest's shoulder.

"I know I can't expect Whirlaway to win every race," Forest agreed. "But he's never run this poorly!"

"Can we go see him?" Dink asked.

"Sure," Forest said, checking his watch. "Meet us back here in about fifteen minutes, okay?"

The kids clambered down the grandstand steps and ran toward the barns. They entered barn E and walked past curious horses peering from stalls.

"There's Whirlaway," Josh said, pointing. The horse, slick with sweat, was tied outside stall 21. Sunny was wiping him down with towels.

Sunny looked up and nodded at the kids.

"I'm sorry you didn't win," Ruth Rose said.

"Not as sorry as I am," Sunny muttered. Her outfit was filthy. She had removed her helmet, and her hair hung down, damp and straggly. Where her goggles had been, her face was clean. The rest was smeared with sweat and track grime. Her once shiny black boots were now brown with dust.

Sunny knelt down and began unwinding the tape from Whirlaway's legs. The tape was grimy.

Sunny shook her head as she worked. "Whirlaway was running like a different horse," she said.

She walked away to find a trash can for the soiled tapes, leaving Whirlaway tied to his stall.

"Maybe Whirlaway was just tired," Dink said.

"Maybe," Ruth Rose agreed. "But jockeys can make horses go slower."

Josh looked at Ruth Rose. "You think Sunny made Whirlaway lose the race?"

Ruth Rose shrugged. "I don't know."

Sunny came back and untied Whirl-away. She had to tug him up the ramp. He rolled his eyes as she walked him into the trailer.

Sunny closed and latched the trailer door. Without saying a word, she climbed into the cab and drove away.

"Something weird is definitely going on between Whirlaway and Sunny," Ruth Rose said.

"Whirlaway might just be having a bad day," Dink said.

Ruth Rose looked at her watch.

"We'd better get back," she said.

They started walking toward the viewing stands. Dink noticed a small group of people gathered around a dark horse and its rider. "There's the winner," he said.

"Yeah, Dancer," said Josh.

"I want to get a picture," Ruth Rose said. The kids walked to the winner's circle. They wiggled through the crowd until they were standing next to Dancer.

Dancer's chest and legs were sweaty. The white tape that covered his ankles was dirty. The jockey was dirty, too. He smiled as people took pictures.

A man wearing a cowboy hat and dark glasses reached up and shook the jockey's hand. "Well done, Andy," he said.

"Piece of cake, Mr. Bee," the jockey answered.

"Guys, move closer," Ruth Rose said. "I want to get a picture of you and Dancer."

Dink and Josh stepped over and stood in front of Dancer. Josh giggled when the horse butted him gently in the back.

The jockey flicked the reins, and Dancer put his head between Dink's and Josh's shoulders.

Ruth Rose snapped the picture. Her camera made a whirring noise, letting her know that the roll of film had run out.

Dink looked at his watch. "Come on, guys. They're waiting for us."

They hurried away and found Forest and Uncle Warren in the viewing box.

"How does Whirlaway look?" Forest asked.

"Tired," Josh said. "Sunny loaded him and they took off."

"I guess we'd better leave, too," Forest said. They headed for the parking lot.

Dink, Josh, and Ruth Rose walked behind Forest and Uncle Warren.

Ruth Rose held up her camera. "I can't wait to get my film developed," she whispered. "I think that last picture is a *big* clue!"

CHAPTER 8

"Maybe Whirlaway is sick," Uncle Warren suggested on the way back.

Forest nodded. "I'll call the vet and get him to come over," he said.

The kids sat in back. Josh slept against his pillow with his mouth open. Next to him, Ruth Rose read *Learning to Ride*.

Dink's book was on his lap. He gazed out the window, watching the scenery flash by. The hum of the car's tires made him feel sleepy. His eyes closed.

The next thing Dink heard was his uncle's voice saying, "Almost home, kids."

Dink opened his eyes, blinked, and looked out the window. He recognized the shops just before Forest's driveway.

"There's a photo place," Ruth Rose said. "Can we stop, Forest?"

"Sure thing," Forest said. He pulled up in front of the small shop. A cheerful sign in the window said PHOTO FINISH. ONE HOUR!

Ruth Rose hopped out and ran inside. She was back a minute later. "I got more film," she said.

Josh sat up and looked around. "Where are we?" he asked.

Dink poked his finger at the back of Josh's shirt. "Josh, there's a black smear on your collar."

Josh twisted his shirt around and stretched out the collar. "Yuck!" he said.

"Where did *that* come from?"

"Maybe it's mud from Whirlaway yesterday," Dink suggested.

"Dink," Josh said, "I changed my shirt after we washed him."

"Could you have leaned against wet paint or something at Saratoga?" Ruth Rose asked.

Josh thought for a second. "I don't think so," he said, "and if I had, there'd be more than just a mark on my collar." He shrugged.

Forest made the turn into his

driveway, and a minute later they were home.

"I've got to change my shirt," Josh said when they had all climbed out of the car.

"No! Let's go see if Sunny and Whirlaway are back yet," Ruth Rose said. She gave Dink and Josh a look.

"Great," Forest said. "I'll see if I can get the vet on the phone."

Uncle Warren took Josh's pillow and the books. Dink, Josh, and Ruth Rose headed for the barn. The stall was empty, and Sunny was nowhere to be seen.

"Okay, what's up?" Josh asked Ruth Rose. They sat on hay bales.

"You know that picture I took of you guys with Dancer?" Ruth Rose asked. "Well, I think someone else was in it. Mr. Bunks!"

Both boys looked blank.

"The man in the sunglasses and

cowboy hat was Mr. Bunks!" Ruth Rose said.

"Are you sure?" Dink asked. "I thought that guy was the horse's owner."

"I think I recognized his big belt buckle from yesterday," Ruth Rose said. "I took a picture so we could be sure."

"Well, if it was him, why didn't Mr. Bunks tell Forest that he was going to be at Saratoga, too?" Dink asked.

"That's what I want to know," Ruth Rose said. "And why did he say he was out of the racing business?"

"Maybe Mr. Bunks doesn't own Dancer," Josh said. "He might have been there like us, just to see the winner up close."

"But he and the jockey knew each other," Ruth Rose said.

Dink nodded. "If that *was* Mr. Bunks at Saratoga," he said, "he is *definitely* hiding something!"

CHAPTER 9

Just then Uncle Warren walked into the barn. He was wearing flip-flops and a bathing suit and carrying a towel.

"Coming for a swim?" he asked.

"Sure," Dink said. The kids followed Uncle Warren toward the house.

"After we swim, let's go get my film," Ruth Rose said quietly.

The kids changed and joined Forest and Uncle Warren in the pool. They played keep-away with a plastic ball.

"Still no sign of Sunny and Whirl-away," Forest said, nodding toward the barn. "I sure hope they didn't have any trouble on the road.".

"We're going to get my film," Ruth Rose said. "Maybe she'll be here when we get back."

"There's a safe bike path on the side of the road," Forest said. "Have a nice walk."

The kids dried off, pulled on their clothes, and headed across the lawn.

"I wonder what's taking Sunny so long to get back here?" Dink asked as they hiked down the driveway.

"She could have stopped for food," Josh said. He rubbed his belly.

A few minutes later, they walked into Photo Finish. Josh immediately spied a rack of candy, so he bought a bag of M&M's.

Ruth Rose's film was ready. She paid the clerk, and they started walking back to Forest's, where they could look at the pictures in private.

Josh ripped open his candy and

began munching, one piece at a time.

When they got back to Forest's, the kids headed straight to the barn. Sunny and Whirlaway had still not returned.

Ruth Rose opened the packet of pictures and took them out. There were a few of her cat, then the one taken by the train conductor.

The next pictures were of horses and the barn at Saratoga. Then there was one of the horses on the track, but it was blurry. Next was Sunny with Whirlaway in barn E.

The last picture was taken at the winner's circle. It showed Dink and Josh with Dancer's head between them. The man in the cowboy hat was standing in the background. He was wearing a leather belt with a big silver buckle.

"It's Mr. Bunks, all right," Dink said.

The kids studied the picture. Ruth Rose brought it closer to her eyes.

"Guys, do you see anything weird about Dancer's forehead?" she asked.

"It looks shiny," Dink said, peering closely.

"And darker than the rest of his face," Josh observed.

"From a distance, you'd never notice," Ruth Rose said.

"What could make it look like that?" asked Dink.

"Something dark, like shoe polish," Josh said.

"Wait a minute," Ruth Rose said. "Josh, let's see that mark on your shirt."

Josh leaned in so Dink and Ruth Rose could inspect his collar.

"It looks like shoe polish," said Dink.

"Yes!" Josh said. "Now I remember! Ruth Rose, when you took our picture, I felt Dancer nudge me in the back."

"So *Dancer* made that mark!" Ruth Rose said.

"But why would anyone want to put shoe polish on a horse?" Dink asked.

"I don't know, but I know who could have done it," Ruth Rose said. "Sunny was polishing her boots with black polish right before the race!"

"But Sunny doesn't have anything to do with Dancer," Josh pointed out.

Ruth Rose shuffled through the pictures until she found the one of Sunny and Whirlaway in barn E. She looked at it for a second, then placed it next to the one of Dink and Josh with Dancer.

"Wow," Josh said. "The horses look like twins!"

Dink picked up the picture of Sunny in barn E. "Except this one has a white mark on his forehead."

"The shoe polish could be covering

up a white mark on Dancer's forehead," Ruth Rose said.

"But why would Sunny, or Mr.
Bunks, or *anybody* want to cover up a
white mark on Dancer's forehead? Why
would it matter?" Josh asked.

Dink thought about that. Then he
remembered Sunny's comment after
the race, about how she felt like she
was riding a different horse. "That's *it*!"
Dink said, snapping his fingers.

"What's what?" Josh asked.

"Guys, what if the horse we washed
wasn't Whirlaway?" Dink asked.

"What do you mean?" asked Josh.

"I mean, what if someone stole
Whirlaway, then brought back a different horse to replace him?"

Josh and Ruth Rose just stared at
Dink.

"Well, that would explain why he
acted so strange," Ruth Rose finally
said.

"And why he blew the race," Josh said.

"It would also explain the shoe polish," said Dink.

"Huh?" said Josh.

"Well," Dink said, "why would someone want to steal a fast racehorse like Whirlaway?"

"To win races!" Ruth Rose said.

"Right," said Dink. "And if someone *did* steal Whirlaway and enter him in a race, he'd be sure to disguise him somehow."

"Like covering up the mark on his forehead with shoe polish!" said Josh.

"So that's why Mr. Bunks was there," Ruth Rose said. "He must have stolen Whirlaway and entered him in the race as Dancer."

"And I'll bet Sunny's working for him," Josh said. "It would have been easy for her to switch the horses."

"Plus, we saw her with shoe polish," Dink said.

"I'd like to ask Sunny a few questions," Ruth Rose said.

"Where *is* Sunny?" Josh asked.

"Good question," said Ruth Rose, looking around the empty barn. She sighed.

"And if she did switch horses, how can we prove the horse she rode in the race wasn't Whirlaway?" Dink asked.

"I know a way," Josh said. He reached into his pocket and pulled out a sugar cube. "Forest said Whirlaway doesn't like sugar. When Sunny gets back, I'll offer this to Whirlaway—or whoever it is. If he eats the sugar, we'll *know* it's not Whirlaway!"

CHAPTER 10

"You're a genius!" Ruth Rose said.

"I know," Josh said.

Dink glanced around the empty barn. "Now all we have to do is wait for Sunny."

Ruth Rose stuffed the pictures back into the packet. "Well, I, for one, am not waiting around," she said. "Come on, let's go check out Mr. Bunks's place again."

"What are we gonna do when we get there?" Josh asked as they hurried up Forest's driveway.

"Look for Whirlaway," Ruth Rose

said. "Do you still have those sugar cubes?"

Josh patted his pocket. "Yep."

The kids cut behind Forest's barn and headed for the logging road.

A few minutes later, they reached Mr. Bunks's house and barn.

"I don't see that dog anywhere," Josh whispered.

"And I don't see Mr. Bunks's truck," Dink said.

"Let's check out the barn," Ruth Rose said. The kids slipped into the barn. It was quiet and dim, with a little light coming through the dusty windows.

"Biscuit's gone!" Dink said, stopping in front of her empty stall. "Where is she?"

As if in answer, they heard a horse whinny. "Come on," Dink said, heading outside.

Behind the barn was an open field

with a path leading through the tall weeds. The kids followed the trail and entered a stand of trees. As they reached the far side of the trees, the kids stopped and stared. They were in a clearing in front of a long shed. A horse trailer was partially hidden behind the low building.

The kids pulled open the wide shed door and peeked inside. Dink wrinkled his nose at the sharp manure smell.

Half of the shed was fenced off with boards. Behind the fence was Biscuit, staring at the newcomers.

In a separate stall next to Biscuit's was another horse, wearing a halter. The dark horse looked just like Whirlaway, except that there was no white diamond on this horse's shiny forehead.

"It's the horse who won," Josh breathed.

"Is it Whirlaway?" Dink whispered.

Josh unwrapped a sugar cube, walked over to the fence, and held out his hand. The dark horse stepped closer for a sniff. Then he snorted and shook his head.

"He won't take it!" Josh exclaimed. He reached out and carefully touched the horse's forehead. When he brought his hand away, his fingers were smeared with something black.

Dink took a towel from a nail on the wall. Holding the horse's halter with one hand, he wiped his forehead.

More black came off, revealing part of a white diamond shape.

Dink felt goose bumps crawl up his back. "Sunny did switch horses!" he said.

"This is Whirlaway," Ruth Rose said. She opened her envelope of pictures. She found the one of Sunny and the horse in barn E and held it up next to the real Whirlaway. "The horse back at

Forest's place is his double!" she said.

"We have to tell Forest!" Josh said.

"Tell him what?" a voice said.

The kids whirled around. In the shed doorway stood Mr. Bunks and Buster. Mr. Bunks was still wearing the clothes he'd worn in the winner's circle, including the silver belt buckle. "Sit, dog," Mr. Bunks said to Buster. The dog sat at his master's side. A low growl came from deep in his throat.

"So you figured it out," Mr. Bunks said. He nodded at the towel in Dink's hand. "Even my boot polish trick."

His boot polish trick? Dink thought. Suddenly Dink realized the truth. Sunny had not been the one to put the boot polish on Whirlaway! It was Mr. Bunks! And it had been Bunks's belt buckle that made the mark in the mud on the horse they washed! It wasn't Sunny who had stolen Whirlaway. She thought she was riding Whirlaway in

the race. Mr. Bunks had done it alone!

Dink glanced around the dim shed, looking for another way out. The windows were closed and too high up.

"Now, if you'll just pass me those pictures," Mr. Bunks said, holding out a hand. The man smiled, but it wasn't the friendly smile he'd shown yesterday.

Dink took the photos from Ruth Rose and handed them to Mr. Bunks.

"We don't need the pictures," Dink said. "We know this is Whirlaway and we know you stole him from Mr. Evans."

Mr. Bunks laughed. "Whirlaway? I don't know what you're talking about," he said. "I bought this horse. Can I help it if he just happens to look like Whirlaway? Can I help it if he just happens to run like the wind?"

He slipped the photos inside his shirt. "No one will ever prove I stole this horse from Forest."

"We won't have to prove anything, Tinker," a voice said. "Not with all these witnesses."

Forest, Uncle Warren, and Sunny walked into the shed.

* * *

An hour later, everyone sat around Forest's picnic table eating burgers.

"How did you guys know where we were?" Dink asked.

"I was coming back just as you were leaving," Sunny said. "You had such determined looks on your faces, I decided to tell Forest."

"And we reached the shed in time to hear everything," Forest said. "Mr. Bunks is going to jail."

"Did Mr. Bunks actually think he could get away with this?" Ruth Rose said.

Forest nodded. "Well, he was lucky to find Whirlaway's double. Even the white face diamonds are the same," he said. "I was fooled, but Sunny noticed a difference."

"Whirlaway is usually so friendly," Sunny said. "I got suspicious when the look-alike acted like he didn't know me. On the way home from Saratoga, I stopped at the vet's. He took a blood sample that'll prove the horse I rode isn't Whirlaway."

"That horse is called Dancer," Forest said. "Bunks switched names, too. Turns out the woman he bought Dancer from didn't treat her horse very well. That's why he was afraid of Sunny. Her voice reminded him of his abusive owner."

"What will happen to Dancer and Biscuit when Mr. Bunks goes to jail?" Ruth Rose asked.

Forest winked. "I've arranged to buy them," he said. "From now on, Whirlaway won't have to run away to visit his mother."

"Awesome!" Josh said. He picked up his hamburger and took a big bite. As he did, a glob of ketchup squirted out and landed on his clean white T-shirt.

A to Z Mysteries

Dear Readers,

One of the most interesting parts of writing the A to Z series has been selecting ideas and words for titles. Some titles have come easily, such as *The Absent Author* and *The Deadly Dungeon*. But other titles are much harder to come up with, such as those for the Q book and the future X book.

Some of you have helped by sending me your ideas, and I do appreciate that. The title *The Invisible Island* came from a reader in Ohio.

Coming up with the R title was fun. After all, my name is Ron Roy, and one of my fictional friends is Ruth Rose. As I began to think about the R book, I made a list of some of my favorite R words. Here's a short list. Maybe you can add some of your own favorite R things.

RABBIT—what's cuter than a bunny?
RACCOON—I love their little hands
RAIN FOREST—great sights, smells, and sounds
RAINY DAY—I stay inside and read!
RASPBERRY—ice cream!
RED—like roses and robins' breasts
REDWOODS—so awesome to see
REINDEER—how else would Santa get here?
RELAXING—with a good mystery book!
RICH—I feel rich because I have good friends
ROCKET—blast off to outer space!
RUBBER BAND—what a super invention!
RUNNING—one of my favorite ways to get exercise

And, of course, the most special R word is **READING**!

I hope you enjoyed reading *The Runaway Racehorse*. It was fun doing the research. I even visited the racetrack in Saratoga Springs, New York. I met a nice worker who showed me the huge green barns and the private viewing boxes.

Nicholas and Eric Oliverio

Here's a picture of me with the Alphabet Zweepstakes winner, Nicholas Oliverio, and his brother, Eric, at lunch in New York City! We had a great time!

Happy reading!

Sincerely,

Ron Roy

Collect clues with Dink, Josh, and Ruth Rose in their next exciting adventure,

THE SCHOOL SKELETON

"Miss Shotsky, where's Mr. Bones?"

The nurse had her back to Dink. "Right there, where he always is," she said.

Dink stared at the empty corner. The school skeleton had hung there as long as Dink could remember. But now the only thing Dink saw in the corner was a red scarf hanging on a hook. "He's not there," Dink said.

Miss Shotsky looked. Her mouth dropped open. "Well, I'll be hog-tied," she said. "He *is* gone!"